First published 2000 in *The Macmillan Treasury of Nursery Stories*
This collection first published 2010 by Macmillan Children's Books
a division of Macmillan Publishers Limited
20 New Wharf Road, London N1 9RR
Basingstoke and Oxford
Associated companies throughout the world
www.panmacmillan.com

ISBN: 978-0-230-74995-5

MACMILLAN CHILDREN'S BOOKS

The Little Mermaid

and other stories

Retold by
Mary Hoffman

Illustrated by
Anna Currey

The Little Mermaid

In the middle of the furthest ocean, where the waters are deepest, live the Mer-people. Their home is beautiful with gardens and flowers, and the only difference between our landscape and this seascape is that fishes dart between the trees instead of birds.

The ancient palace of the Mer-king was made of coral, with amber windows and a roof of mussel shells, which opened and shut in the rippling water. The Mer-king himself had six beautiful daughters but no wife to help manage them. The Mer-princesses' mother had died years before and the household was managed by the king's mother.

Each princess had her own little garden and some were decorated with trophies from shipwrecks. The youngest princess, who was the most beautiful, had rescued the marble statue of a boy from a wrecked ship and put it in the middle of her garden. She was a quiet child and liked to sit and gaze at her statue.

She was very interested in humans and always eager

to hear what her grandmother had to tell her about life above the waves. As each princess reached the age of fifteen, she was allowed to visit the world above the sea, and the little mermaid couldn't wait for her turn.

When it was time for her oldest sister to swim above, the little mermaid was very excited and eager to hear all the news. When her sister returned, full of stories of the town she could see from the shore, its lights and music and the sound of its church bells, no one listened more intently than the youngest princess.

And so it was for the next five years, as each sister swam up to the surface and came back with stories of clouds and birds and ships and icebergs. The little mermaid felt that her turn would never come.

But of course, it did. On the evening of her fifteenth birthday, her grandmother called her over and adorned her hair with a wreath of white lilies made from pearls. To be truthful, the little mermaid would have preferred a simple garland of red flowers from her garden, but she understood that a princess must look grand at all times.

She said goodbye to all her sisters and rose alone through the blue waters of the ocean. The sun was setting as she broke through the surface of the water, and the sky was streaked with gold and rose. The evening star was shining and the sea was still as a looking-glass.

A large three-masted sailing ship was moving calmly through the ocean and the little mermaid could hear sweet music coming from it. As the sky grew dark, dozens of little lamps were lit on deck and coloured flags fluttered in the slight breeze. The mermaid thought she had never seen anything prettier.

So she swam closer and looked through the portholes.

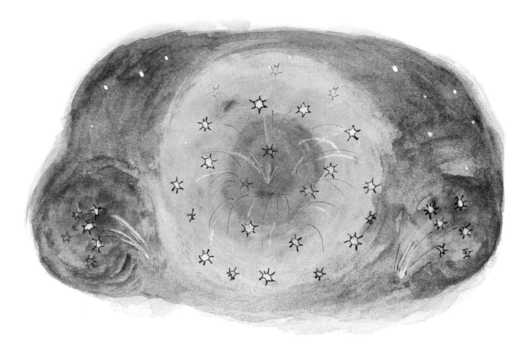

There she saw a merry party of men dressed in rich velvets and satins, such as she had never seen. The handsomest of all was a young man not more than sixteen, and it seemed to be his birthday. Soon, all the men went up on deck and fireworks were let off. At first, the noise and gunpowdery smells terrified the mermaid and she hid under the water, but her curiosity got the better of her and then she thought she had never seen anything so wonderful. The whole sky was alight with green and gold and purple stars.

The little mermaid watched late until the party was over and everyone had gone to bed. Then she looked through the cabin porthole of the young man (who was, in fact, a prince) and gazed on him while he slept. His lovely face reminded her of her marble statue, but was made more beautiful by the colour in his lips and cheeks and the breath that stirred a feather on his pillow.

As the little mermaid followed the prince's ship, the waters below her began to heave and the sky to darken. A fierce wind whipped the waves into tall peaks and the rain fell heavily from the sky. The little mermaid loved it, especially when the ship went up and down in the water and the waves towered over it.

But the crew felt very differently. They scrambled to furl the sails, but they couldn't save the ship. It was struck by a huge wave and cracked in two. For the first time, the little mermaid realised that her prince was in danger.

She swam to the sinking ship, weaving between the broken spars, and looked everywhere for the young man. Then, a flash of lightning illuminated the scene, and she saw the prince clinging to a piece of wood. She swam to his side and pulled him out of the way of the ship,

which was now disappearing under the waves, taking many sailors with it.

The prince was half-dead, his eyes closed, and unaware of his rescuer, who held him in her arms till daybreak. When the sun came up, the little mermaid saw that they were near an island and swam towards the woody shore.

There was a little bay, where a river ran down to the sea, and the mermaid swam into it and pushed the prince onto the sandy shore, turning his face to the sun. But, of course, she couldn't get far out of the water because of her tail. As soon as she had done what she could for him, she hid among some reeds.

As the sun climbed higher, a group of girls came down from a white building to bathe in the river. The little

mermaid heard their exclamations as they found the prince. Their leader, a tall young woman, revived him and the little mermaid had the satisfaction of seeing him awake and speak, but then she became afraid of so many humans so near to her and dived back to her home beneath the waves.

But she could not forget the prince. She spent all her time in her garden, talking to her statue, until her family were quite worried about her. Eventually she told her secret to one of her sisters, who passed it on to the others.

They were all very sympathetic and told her they knew the country where the prince lived. They even took her to see his castle. From then on, she spent hours watching the castle and occasionally caught a glimpse of the prince.

Whenever she was under the water, she thought how dull her home looked, with its colours all blue and green and mauve, and she longed for the bright yellow of daffodils and sunshine and golden crowns.

The little mermaid wanted to know all she could about humans, so she went to her grandmother and asked, "If they do not drown, do human beings live forever?"

"No, my child," said her grandmother. "They all die, and they don't even live anything like as long as we do. We, as you know, live three hundred years. But then, sadly, we are turned to foam and cannot remain with our loved ones."

"What happens to humans, then?" asked the little mermaid.

"Their souls go on living after their bodies die," said her grandmother. "And in their heaven they are reunited with those they have loved on earth."

"Oh, how beautiful!" cried the little mermaid. "I should give up my three hundred years for one day as a human if I could have an immortal soul."

"Don't be so silly," said her grandmother. "We are far happier than humans are and enjoy our lives more than they do."

"Then is there no way," asked the little mermaid, "that a mer-person could get a human soul?"

"Well, there is," said her grandmother, reluctantly. "But it never happens. If a mermaid could get a human man to promise to love her and take her in marriage, then she would get a share of his soul. But the reason it won't happen is that the feature we admire most—our fine tails —is to humans most repulsive. They want a body to finish in two ugly pillars, which they call legs."

This gave the little mermaid lots to think about and, from then on, she was determined to get a pair of legs and make the prince love her as she loved him. There was an enchantress living under the sea, of whom all the mermaids were afraid, for she lived in a castle of human

bones in the middle of a boiling whirlpool.

But now the little mermaid determined to go and see her. She braved the bog and the trees made of living coils which snatched at passers-by, and made her way to the enchantress' throne. The sea-witch sat with a toad in her lap, caressing it as a fine lady would her cat.

"I know what you want," she told the little mermaid. "And you can have it, but at a price."

When the little mermaid heard what she would have to do to get legs, she nearly fainted.

"First, you must give up your beautiful voice to me," said the witch. "No more singing or even speaking for you."

The little mermaid agreed, though she was sad that her prince would never hear her silvery singing voice.

"Next, you must know that if I take away your tail and give you legs, the moment of transformation will be like having your tail cut in half by a sword. And every step you take upon the land will be like walking on knives."

"I would do anything for my prince," said the little mermaid, bravely.

"Very well," said the witch. "Now, finally, you must know that if the prince doesn't come to love you enough to marry you, then the morning after he marries another, your heart will break and you will turn into foam upon the sea. Are you sure that the slim chance of an immortal soul is worth all this suffering?"

"Yes," said the little mermaid. "My prince is worth all of it."

So the witch made her a terrible potion and took her voice away. She told the little mermaid to swim to the shore and drink the potion there.

The little mermaid swam away over her own palace, where all her family lay sleeping, and far away, carrying the phial, to the palace of the prince. There, she pulled herself up onto the shore and boldly drank the whole potion in one go.

Immediately, the terrible pains started in her tail. How she suffered as it split and shrank and she grew two slender legs in its place.

She shed a silent tear or two as she saw her glittery silver scales disappear. When she tried to stand, she thought the pain would kill her. Slowly, she dragged her unfamiliar legs, in spite of the sensation of walking on knives, until she found herself on the marble steps of the palace, where she fell into a swoon.

By then, it was morning and the palace guards found her. She was dressed in nothing but her long hair and some seaweed, but she was so beautiful that they were sure the prince would want to see her. So they took her to the housekeeper to be washed and dressed and then she was taken to the prince.

He was enchanted by her, though she could speak not a word, and asked her to dance with him. Imagine, if it caused her pain to walk, what agony it was for her to dance! But the little mermaid moved as gracefully as the waves and everyone admired her.

Soon she was the prince's firm favourite and she was as happy as could be. But, as time went by, he showed no signs of wanting to marry her. In fact, he began to treat her as if she were a pretty toy or a favourite pet.

The little mermaid asked the prince with her eyes if he loved her, and he understood and said, "Oh, I do love you, little one. You are so sweet and pretty. You remind me of a lovely maiden who rescued me from drowning. I was cast up on an island after a shipwreck and there was a temple full of maidens. One of them saved my life and sent me back to my country and I have dreamed of her ever since. You are a bit like her and, since I shall never find her again, you must be my comfort."

The little mermaid's eyes filled with unshed tears. He didn't even know that it was she who had saved him!

Next day, she heard the courtiers talking of the prince's forthcoming marriage to the daughter of a neighbouring king, but she didn't believe them.

But that night, the prince said to her as he curled a lock of her hair between his fingers, "I must go and see this princess my parents want me to marry. But she can't look as much like that temple maiden as you do, so I shan't marry her. Will you come with me? You aren't afraid of the sea, are you?" And the little mermaid shook her head and smiled.

But when they reached the land where the foreign princess lived, she became uneasy, for she recognised the shore. And indeed, as soon as the prince saw the princess, he recognised her.

"It is she, the temple maiden who saved my life!" he told his little companion. "Come, you must be happy for me—I know how fond of me you are."

And the little mermaid nodded, but her heart was hurting even more than her legs, which was an old pain she was used to. This new pain came from the knowledge that her prince would marry someone else and she would never gain an immortal soul.

The next day, the prince and his princess were married and he brought his bride on board his ship, a ship very like the one that the little mermaid had first seen him on. Again, there were lights and music and fireworks, but how different they seemed to the little mermaid. She leaned on the rail, knowing that at the first rays of the rising sun, she would be turned into foam.

Looking down in the water, she suddenly saw her five sisters swimming alongside the ship. But they were different; their lovely long hair was all cut off.

"We gave it to the sea-witch!" they cried, "in return for a spell to save you. You must take this dagger and plunge it into the prince's heart before daybreak. Then let his warm blood fall on your feet and your mermaid's tail will be restored. Then you can live with us for your full three hundred years. But you must act before morning; either you or he must die. Farewell! Then they plunged under the waves.

The mermaid took the dagger they had given her and went into the prince's cabin. She saw him sleeping peacefully and she knew she could never hurt him. She ran to the edge of the ship and

threw the dagger
in the water. Just then,
the red beams of the rising
sun streaked the sky. With a
voiceless cry, the little mermaid
leapt over the edge of the ship and
felt herself dissolving into foam.

But, as she sank below the
water, she saw the sky filled with
transparent beings, with sweet melodious
voices. They swept down and took the
little mermaid up with them and she saw
that she had become as transparent as
they were. They were spirits of the air
and they gave her her
voice back.

So the mermaid went singing through the air with her companions. She was able to swoop down and kiss her prince, unseen, as he looked sorrowfully over the side of the ship for her. Then she travelled through the air for three hundred years, with the spirits, doing good deeds and bringing happiness everywhere.

And, because she had loved so much and so hard, at the end of that time she won an immortal soul for herself, long after the prince and his descendants were turned to dust.

Goldilocks and the Three Bears

Once upon a time there were three bears who lived together in a pretty cottage in the middle of a forest. One was a Great Huge Bear with a deep gruff voice, another was a Middle-Sized Bear with a low tuneful voice and the third was a Small Wee Bear with a high squeaky voice. They each had a bed, a chair and a porridge-bowl of exactly the right size to suit each one of them.

One day, after they had made their breakfast porridge, they went for a walk in the forest, to let it cool down so that it would not burn their mouths. And while they were away, a little girl called Goldilocks came tripping up the path to their front door.

She had been walking in the forest without telling her parents, which was very naughty. She had lost her way chasing butterflies and one particularly handsome red and yellow one had led her to the bears' house. Of course she didn't know it belonged to three bears, but by then she was very hungry, so she knocked on the door. There was no answer, so she lifted the latch and stepped inside.

Goldilocks found herself in the nicest kitchen, with a stone floor, a big iron cooking range and a comfortable tabby cat sleeping on a rag rug. On the scrubbed wooden table, Goldilocks found three bowls of porridge, with three spoons beside them. She couldn't help herself; she hadn't had any breakfast. She dipped a spoon into the biggest bowl and took a taste.

"Oh!" cried Goldilocks, "I can't eat that—it's much too hot."

Then she tried the porridge in the middle-sized bowl.

"Ugh!" cried Goldilocks, "I can't eat that—it's much too cold!"

Then she tried the smallest bowl.

"Yum, yum!" said Goldilocks. "Not too hot and not too cold. It's just right!"

And she ate it all up.

In the kitchen were three armchairs. Goldilocks went and sat in the biggest one.

"I don't like this chair," she said, wriggling her bottom. "It's much too hard."

So she tried the middle-sized chair.

"I don't like this one either," said Goldilocks. "It's much too soft."

So she jumped off that one, too. And then she sat in the smallest chair. "Aah!" sighed Goldilocks. "Not too hard

and not too soft. It's just right." And she
snuggled so hard into the smallest
chair that it broke in pieces!

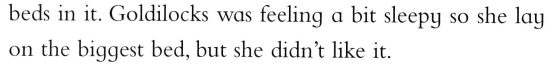

"Oops!" said Goldilocks
and decided to explore
upstairs. She found a
cosy bedroom with three
beds in it. Goldilocks was feeling a bit sleepy so she lay
on the biggest bed, but she didn't like it.

"The blankets are much too heavy," said Goldilocks
and she climbed into the middle-sized bed.

"The covers are much too light," she complained and
put herself into the smallest bed.

"Lovely!" said Goldilocks. "This duvet is not too heavy
and not too light. It's just right."

And she curled up all cosily in the
smallest bed and fell fast asleep.

Now, the three bears who
lived in the little cottage were
coming back from their walk.
As soon as they got into their
kitchen, the Great Huge Bear
looked at his bowl and

growled in his deep gruff voice, "Who's been eating my porridge?"

The Middle-Sized Bear looked at her bowl and sighed in her low tuneful voice, "Who's been eating my porridge?"

And the Small Wee Bear took one look at his bowl and squeaked in his little high voice, "Who's been eating my porridge?—and has eaten it all up!"

The Great Huge Bear sat down. "Who's been sitting in my chair?" he growled in his deep gruff voice.

The Middle-Sized Bear sat down. "Who's been sitting in my chair?" she sighed in her low tuneful voice.

And the Small Wee Bear couldn't sit down at all. "Who's been sitting in my chair?" he squeaked in his little high voice, "and has broken it all in pieces!"

The three bears went upstairs. The Great Huge Bear looked at his bed. "Who's been sleeping in my bed?" he growled in his deep gruff voice.

The Middle-Sized Bear looked at her bed. "Who's been sleeping in my bed?" she

sighed in her low tuneful voice.

And the Small Wee Bear looked at his bed and squeaked in his little high voice, "Who's been sleeping in my bed? And is *still* sleeping in my bed? There's a little girl in my bed!"

In her sleep Goldilocks heard the Great Huge Bear's voice like the sound of a deep buzz saw in the forest, then the Middle-Sized Bear's voice like leaves sighing in an autumn wind and then the Small Wee Bear's voice like the high-pitched squeaking of a family of mice. And when she heard the high-pitched squeaking, she sat bolt upright in the bed.

And what should she see but three furry brown bears looking down at her! She sprang out of bed and ran towards the open window. Goldilocks was so afraid of the bears though, to tell the truth, they were very mild and gentle ones, that she jumped right out of the window. Luckily it wasn't a long drop, so she was able to run off home.

The bears scratched their heads and went back downstairs to make a fresh pot of porridge. They never found out who Goldilocks was and they never saw her again.

The Sun
and the Wind

The sun and the wind were always arguing about who was stronger and more powerful. One day, they decided to put it to the test. They saw a man walking along the road, who was wearing a fine new cloak.

"Whichever one of us can get that cloak off him," said the wind, "must be the more powerful, don't you think?"

"Definitely," said the sun. "You go first."

So the wind took a deep breath and puffed and blew until the poor man could scarcely stagger along the road. But the colder and windier it got, the more the man wrapped his warm cloak around him. The wind tugged at it and did his best to pull the cloak away, but the man clutched it ever harder.

"I think it's my turn, now," said the sun.

He shone with his most glorious beams on the man, who soon became quite warm. As he walked along the road, the hot sun made him sweat, so he unwrapped his cloak, unfastened it and, finally, he was feeling so warm that he had to take it off and sling it over his shoulder.

"Ha!" said the sun. "Who is the more powerful?" And the wind had to agree that the sun had succeeded where he had failed.

Which only goes to show that, if you want someone to do something, a warm smile can be more effective than bullying.